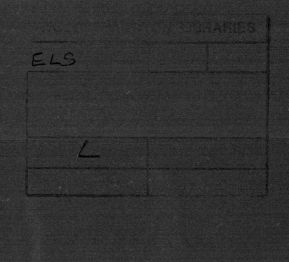

First experiences
Big bed

W
FRANKLIN WATTS
NEW YORK • LONDON • SYDNEY

"Wake up, Milly," said Mum. "Your new bed is here."

"Can Teddy have a new bed too?" asked Milly.

Mum unpacked the big boxes.

"I've got just the right box for
Teddy's bed," said Milly.

"I can't find the hammer. Can you see it anywhere?" frowned Mum.

Mum twisted the screws into the wood. "Oh, dear!" she said, "this is hard work."

Milly was very busy gluing Teddy's new bed.

"Phew, your new bed is ready now," said Mum at last.

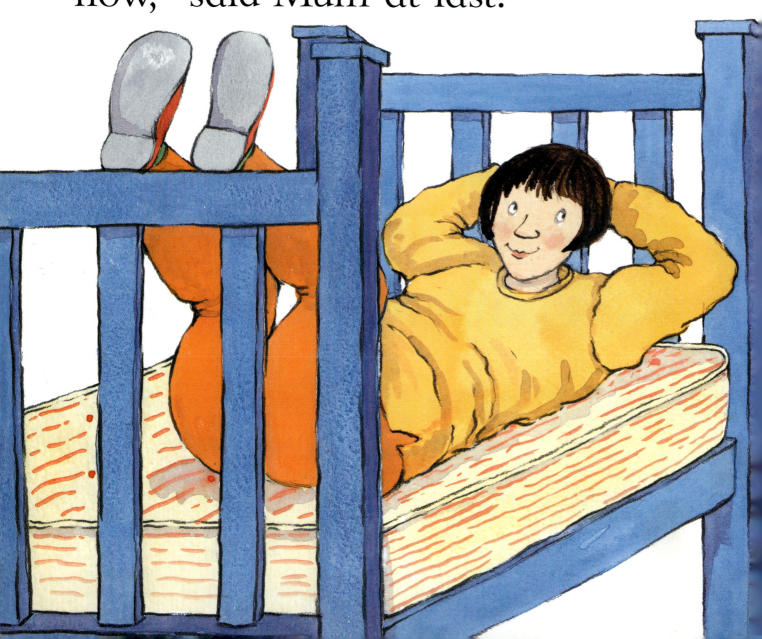

"So is Teddy's," Milly smiled proudly.

Milly had great fun bouncing on her big bed.

"Isn't it BIG!" said Milly.
"I can't wait for it to be night."

"Mum, Teddy wants to know if he can have a story in his new bed?"

"Of course he can," smiled Mum.
"Would you like to help him
to choose one?"

Milly and Teddy snuggled down
in their new beds.

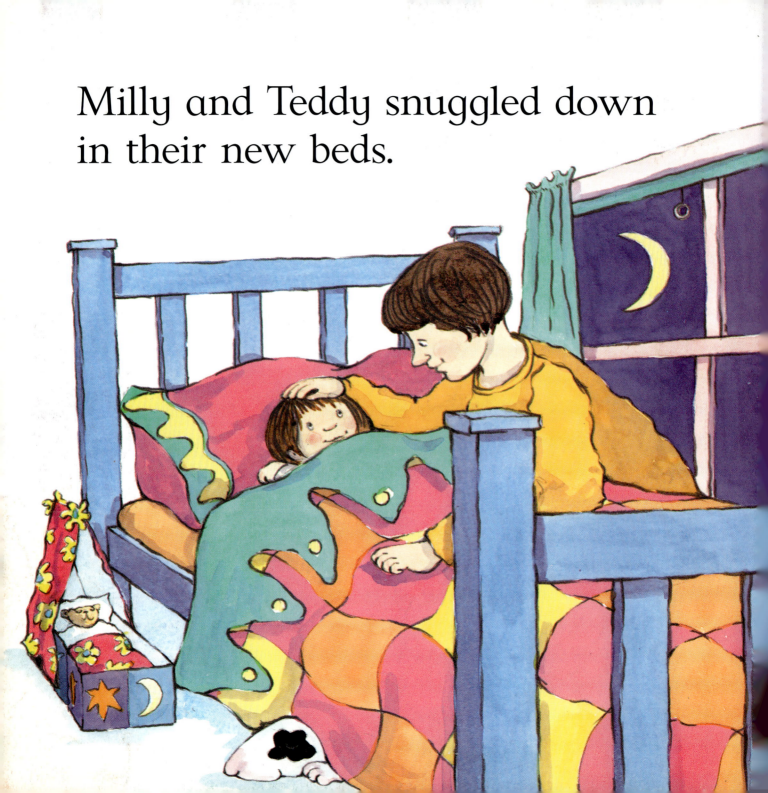

Goodnight, Milly.
Goodnight, Teddy.

Make a bed for your Teddy.

Find a shoe box and
a long piece of card.

Decorate the box and the card
with paint or sticky shapes.

Fold the card in half and
then open it out again.

Glue the edges of the card to one end of your box. Then leave it to dry.

Now you can snuggle your Teddy into his new bed. Find some bits of material for blankets.

Sharing books with your child

Early Worms are a range of books for you to share with your child. Together you can look at the pictures and talk about the subject or story. Listening, looking and talking are the first vital stages in children's reading development, and lay the early foundation for good reading habits.

Talking about the pictures is the first step in involving children in the pages of a book, especially if the subject or story can be related to their own familiar world. When children can relate the matter in the book to their own experience, this can be used as a starting point for introducing new knowledge, whether it is counting, getting to know colours or finding out how other people live.

Gradually children will develop their listening and concentration skills as well as a sense of what a book is. Soon they will learn how a book works: that you turn the pages from right to left, and read the story from left to right on a double page. They start to realize that the black marks on the page have a meaning and that they relate to the pictures. Once children have grasped these basic essentials they will develop strategies for "decoding" the text such as matching words and pictures, and recognising the rhythm of the language in order to predict what comes next. Soon they will start to take over the role of an independent reader, handling and looking at books even if they can't yet read the words.

Most important of all, children should realize that books are a source of pleasure. This stems from your reading sessions which are times of mutual enjoyment and shared experience. It is then that children find the key to becoming real readers.

First published in 1997
This edition published 2000
by Franklin Watts
96 Leonard Street,
London EC2A 4XD

Franklin Watts Australia
14 Mars Road
Lane Cove
NSW 2066

Text copyright
© Lisa Bruce 1997, 2000
Illustrations copyright
© Susie Jenkin-Pearce 1997, 2000

Series editor: Paula Borton
Art director: Robert Walster

Photography Steve Shott
With thanks to Ben Ridley-Johnson

A CIP catalogue record for this
book is available from the British
Library.

ISBN 0 7496 2729 8 (hbk)
ISBN 0 7496 3493 6 (pbk)

Dewey Classification 649

Printed in Belgium

Consultant advice: Sue Robson and Alison Kelly, Senior Lecturers in Education,
Faculty of Education, Early Childhood Centre, Roehampton Institute, London.

Paperback titles in this series:

Pets	Weather	Who are you?	Time	First Experiences
Guinea Pig	Windy day	In the Sea	Morning time	New shoes
0 7496 3498 7	0 7496 3497 9	0 7496 3510 X	0 7496 3487 1	0 7496 3492 8
Kitten	Snowy day	In the Polar Lands	Play time	A party
0 7496 3499 5	0 7496 3495 2	0 7496 3511 8	0 7496 3488 X	0 7496 3491 X
Puppy	Sunny day	On the Farm	Shopping time	Staying the night
0 7496 3500 2	0 7496 3496 0	0 7496 3512 6	0 7496 3489 8	0 7496 3490 1
Rabbit	Rainy day	In the Rainforest	Bed time	Big bed
0 7496 3501 0	0 7496 3494 4	0 7496 3513 4	0 7496 3486 3	0 7496 3493 6